T0162673

BlackLight:
BEYOND THE DARKNESS

D. J. Kowalenko

iUniverse LLC
Bloomington

BLACKLIGHT:
BEYOND THE DARKNESS

iUniverse books may be ordered through booksellers or by contacting:

iUniverse
1663 Liberty Drive
Bloomington, IN 47403
www.iuniverse.com
1-800-Authors (1-800-288-4677)

Because of the dynamic nature of the Internet, any web addresses or links contained in this book may have changed since publication and may no longer be valid. The views expressed in this work are solely those of the author and do not necessarily reflect the views of the publisher, and the publisher hereby disclaims any responsibility for them.

Any people depicted in stock imagery provided by Thinkstock are models, and such images are being used for illustrative purposes only. Certain stock imagery © Thinkstock.

ISBN: 978-1-4917-3135-2 (sc)
ISBN: 978-1-4917-3134-5 (e)

Library of Congress Control Number: 2014908133

Printed in the United States of America.
iUniverse rev. date: 05/05/2014

In memory of Adam Kowalenko, 1979–2013, my brother, my friend, my supporter. Follow the light.

1. BROKEN REALITY

Each one of us lives in our own reality. But not everyone's reality matters. It's only the ones that are told and believed by a failing system known as the truth that matter.

The musty smell of the air, the dog barking its head off—it all felt like he was home back at the city, but he wasn't. Jason opened his eyes, staring ever so carefully around so as to not get noticed. Only two hours ago, he had been just another guest attending the grand opening of Cosmic City, a massive superbuilding filled to the brim with casinos, shopping malls, booths, and even hospitals. An all-in-one centre built in the middle of Alberta, Canada. He was now lying in a cave located somewhere in Cosmic City, bound by rope and watching a large pirate pace around his brother Brody. The cave was dimly lit, with only the glow from the cave entrance and the flickering light of the fire illuminating the place. They had been kidnapped along with some other tourists by a small group of psychotic people calling themselves pirates. One of them had already been killed and was now roasting over a fire stationed at the centre of the cave. A much scrawnier man was kneeling over and gnawing at the dead guy's shinbone. Jason breathed sharply as he fought the reaction to vomit. Jason turned his gaze over to his brother, who had been struck in the face a few times, evident from the red over his cheekbone and eye and his split lip. Jason gritted his teeth, wanting to stand up and defend his brother. But he couldn't help at all; bound or unbound, Jason was less than useless in a fight. Jason looked over at the dog locked in a wooden kennel. It was a scrawny-looking German shepherd with a dirty coat of fur and a shock collar wrapped tightly around its neck. Jason shook his head, wondering when it would stop barking. He let his view trail over to the two remaining tourists. A mop-headed blond who Jason would've placed in his early twenties, around his own age, and a stunning young woman with raven hair that was done up in a ponytail, which let her bangs hang in her eyes and frame her face. She looked young, maybe only a year or two younger than Jason, and had beautiful, creamy skin. He lingered on her hazel eyes for a moment before shooting a wary look at the large pirate. The man—Brutus, as he was called—had quit pacing and left the cave. Jason didn't know why, but he took the time to crawl slowly over to Brody, who was untying himself as Jason crawled. The scrawny pirate—Mucus, Brutus had called him—was facing the other way and chewing up the thigh of the dead tourist.

"What the hell are you doing?" Jason asked in a panic as his brother untied himself.

"I'm going to get us out of here. I promised Mom that I'd keep you safe," Brody replied as he set the rope behind him. Brody had been through the scouts and other training survival groups before, and he had trained a little in escaping rope with their father before he had passed away.

"Dad was a soldier, remember?" Brody continued. "He taught me a little something about escaping."

The two talked quietly as Brody untied Jason, keeping a sharp watch on the cave entrance and Mucus so they didn't get noticed. The other prisoners simply watched as Brody finished untying Jason, perhaps wondering if Brody would save them as well.

"We're going to get killed!" Jason whined as his ropes were tossed aside.

"We'll die all the same if we sit here!" Brody countered and then gestured to Jason to be quiet. Jason watched as Brody crept his way over to Mucus and wrapped his arm around the cannibal's throat, choking him out with a sleeper hold. Jason knew all too well what Brody's sleeper hold could do, having been playfully victimized by it when they were younger.

◈   ◈   ◈

Brody squeezed the last of the air out of Mucus's lungs and pushed him over. He then took a piece of meat from the storage barrel nearby and tossed it into the dog's pen. The dog went quiet as it wolfed the meat down. Brody unlocked its cage but kept the door closed, gesturing to the dog to stay put. It whined and lay down, licking its lips. Brody then slipped past the entrance, moving over to the other two prisoners. As Jason watched Brody set up his plan, he could hear the echo of Brutus speaking with a sinister-sounding man.

"So, Snake, what—"

"Do *not* call me that. I am boss, and that's it!" the sinister man screamed at Brutus, cutting him off midsentence.

"Right. Sorry, boss …" replied Brutus. Jason pulled his gaze from the cave entrance as Brody finished untying the other two prisoners. Brody then asked for their names.

"I'm Sam … Samuel," the kid replied, his voice catching in his throat.

"Kara," the girl said with a whisper as Brody turned his gaze to her. Jason listened as he watched the entryway with wide, panicked eyes, watching every little movement within his vision. Brody ordered them to return to their positions and hold their wrists together as if tied up. Jason fell over onto his side in the same position he was in before Brutus had left, and Brody lifted his arms above his head again. Brutus walked back into the cave alone and looked over at Mucus, who was slumped over by the fireplace.

"Mucus!" he called to no answer. "Useless thing probably choked to death on some bone," he spat, turning to face Brody again. Jason winced as the man walked up to his brother but saw the man stop in his tracks. Had he noticed the missing ropes? Jason hoped for all their sakes that he hadn't. Brutus stared for a moment and then turned and began walking toward Samuel in a slow, sinister manner, wearing an evil grin on his face.

"You're next," he boomed, pointing with his thumb over his shoulder to the firepit. Sam fidgeted, almost as if deciding to run or fight. Then he stood up and lunged at Brutus. His attempt was futile, as he got stabbed in the gut by a large knife Brutus had quickly drawn. Kara screamed for him, and Brody cursed to himself, standing up behind the man and wrapping him in a tight chokehold. But Brutus was bigger and quickly threw himself back into the cave wall, bashing the air out of Brody and forcing him to let go. Brody fell to the floor, and Brutus made a move for his throat. Jason called out to him, picking up a small, jagged stone and lunging at Brutus, smashing him in the face and cutting the big man just under his left eye. Brutus growled and showed his teeth, turning toward Jason and raising his knife.

"Get him, boy!" Brody managed to call out, and the dog burst free from its cage and chomped hard onto Brutus's forearm. He yelled and threw the dog off with a hard swing and then backed up a few steps, becoming illuminated from the light of the cave entrance. The action stopped as the sound of gunfire filled the cave. Brutus's shoulders slumped, a trail of blood pouring from his forehead. Brutus fell over as a man carrying a smoking 9-mm handgun entered the cave. He also wore a red T-shirt, but he had khaki shorts as opposed to the other two's faded blue jeans. The man whom Brutus had called Snake just outside the cave scratched his short, spiky mohawk as he looked around at everyone. He then lifted the dead Brutus by the collar of his shirt and began screaming at him.

"What the hell, man? I thought I told you to watch them." As he screamed, Brody saw his chance to attack and made a move for Snake. Snake barely glanced over to his right and raised his gun, planting two bullets into Brody's chest. Brody fell backward, and Jason cried out, moving swiftly to his brother's side along with Kara.

"No, you can't die, Brody—not you!" he cried out, pushing his hands onto his brother's wounds. Snake laughed as he dropped Brutus onto the ground.

"Okay, I lost my cool. My fault, bro, but here's what I'm going to do," he said as Jason continued trying to save his brother. "Your name is Jason Rain, right? So here's what I'm going to do: I'm going to let you and your little girlfriend here run. You get 30 seconds starting 20 seconds ago to run!" His voice was beginning to grow excited. "Didn't you hear me? I said run, little piggy—run!" He laughed psychotically, and Jason took Kara's hand, making a beeline out of the cave with her and the dog as Snake laughed.

Snake started to give chase but stopped when he saw the other two members of his group standing up. He looked at Mucus and Brutus, who were standing on either side of him.

"What the hell is this," he asked with a smirk, "some messed-up joke?"

The two growled as their flesh turned dark grey and their veins blackened. Snake continued to smirk and shook his head as he backed up a few steps. Brutus turned to face Snake and let out a loud squeal.

"I killed you once, you weirdo, and I'll do it again!" Snake warned as he aimed his gun. Brutus began shuffling over to him, and Snake opened fire, hitting him twice in the chest and again in the head, dropping the zombified Brutus to the floor. He began to turn toward Mucus but got bit in the forearm. Snake growled and smashed Mucus away and then unloaded two bullets into his head. He then collapsed to the ground, staring up at his brass bracelet, which had a glowing green gem embedded in it.

"God damn it!" he cursed as his eyes closed.

Jason escaped the cave with Kara and the dog, stopping when he saw the mall again. But it was different now. People were running, being chased by crazed zombie-looking people, and screams filled the mall.

"Oh God, oh crap!" he muttered, holding his head

with his hands, his whole body shaking as he had a breakdown.

"Jason?" Kara called, shaking him. Jason stared over at her hazel eyes. His breathing quickened, and his vision went hazy. She shook him again and slapped his face.

"Freak out later. We have to go!" she yelled at him. A blood-chilling squeal from behind Kara grabbed their attention. They turned to see a zombie shuffling toward them at surprising speed. The dog barked and tackled the zombie, pulling it to the floor and going viciously at its throat. The zombie wriggled slowly, stopping only when the dog tore the head free and tossed it aside.

"Oh, good dog," Jason said, petting its head. The three turned to see more zombies coming from behind. Jason once again grabbed Kara's hand and ran with her in the opposite direction. The dog barked at the zombies, but with a whimper it turned and ran beside its newfound masters.

2. I Need a Gun
2. I Need a Gun

Guns, like any weapon, can be used for both defending and murdering people. But no matter which you choose, in the end it's all the same.

The three of them managed to escape the oncoming zombies and hide away in a small convenience booth on the north end of the mall. Jason helped Kara close the steel security fence that the shops used to protect the booths from theft and vandalism. The dog sat down beside Jason and began kicking and scratching at the shock collar. Jason lifted his head from his lap, looked over at the dog, and then called it over.

"Come on, boy, let's get that collar off," he said as he picked up a box knife from the shelf beside him. He stopped for a moment to think about how convenient it was that they were safe in a convenience store that had many things that they needed. He chuckled dryly at the thought and began to cut the collar off of the dog. As he did, Kara stared out of the store and kept watch for zombies.

"We need to give you a name, boy. What about ..." Jason mumbled to the dog as he tossed the collar away, "Sullivan—you like that name, right boy?" The dog tilted its head sideways and stuck its tongue out.

"I knew it," Jason said happily as the dog jumped up, and he scratched its neck and back. Jason then reached out and grabbed a black leather collar off the shelf and put it around Sullivan's neck.

Kara looked over her shoulder at the two and smiled faintly; the dog was good at getting Jason's spirit up, and that was great. She then stared back out at the mall, thinking that she had never seen anything like what was happening either and that in her own way she was freaking out herself. Jason looked over at her and noticed the panic and discomfort hidden behind her eyes and shoved the dog off of him. He then walked over to her and put a hand on her shoulder.

"You okay?" he asked quietly, and she looked over at him.

"Yeah, I'm as okay as I can be," she said reassuringly, but Jason caught the hitch in her voice. Jason had always been on the other end of the consoling, so his skills were rusty at best. He said the only thing that came to his mind at the time.

"We've gotta get out of here, and fast. If we don't escape Cosmic City, we're going to be dead too!" She looked up into his silver-blue eyes and laughed dryly.

"That's comforting … Jason?" she asked, and he nodded. "But do you have a plan?"

"Um …" he mumbled back, looking around at the store. He then stood up and walked a few paces toward the dog, which was watching them with an almost amazed look on its face.

"Aha, I've got it!" Jason said finally, grabbing some things from around the store. He pulled a shopping cart over and began filling it with heavy things, ending with the dog on top. He then tied a triangular snow shovel backward onto the front of it, making a makeshift plow of sorts.

"Convenient, right?" he asked between deep breaths, showcasing the contraption. She smirked at it and stood up. After their first encounter, Kara would've placed Jason as the cry-baby, go-nowhere type, but she could now see potential in him.

"Okay," she said after a few moments of silence

that made Jason nervous. Jason turned the cart to face the entrance of the small shop and Kara opened the steel fence, raising it into the roof. As she did, Jason took out a piece of bubblegum and stuck it into his mouth. The two of them then pushed the now very heavy shopping cart out of the store and pointed it north. They stared for a moment into each other's eyes, reassuring each other, and then turned and pushed it as hard and fast as possible, letting out a loud battle cry to raise their courage up. A zombie noticed them and made a small dash but was slammed aside by the makeshift battering ram, and its side turned into a creamy smear on the front of their cart. Jason and Kara kept on pushing, heading toward the exit as the dog, Sullivan, just sat there and enjoyed the ride, letting his tongue hang loose. The cart suddenly pulled around to the side and tipped over; Sullivan jumped off before it landed on him. Jason and Kara cursed as the loud noise began attracting unwanted attention. The two then ran with Sullivan the rest of the way to the exit. When they arrived, they saw bodies littering the tiled floor and thick steel doors blocking the exit smeared with bloody handprints. Jason ran over and smashed his hand hard on the door.

"No, this can't be happening!" he yelled as he tugged on the door as hard as he could, repeating the word no. Kara leaned heavily on the door, almost ready to break down.

"What kind of a nightmare is this?" she said with a strangled voice, fighting back tears that stung her eyes. Sullivan grabbed their attention by barking at some oncoming zombies. They turned, and Kara instructed Jason to grab the fire axe that was hanging behind some glass by the door. He wrapped his arm up with his jacket and hit the glass hard, cracking it slightly. He hit it again, and the glass broke, allowing him to grab the fire axe.

"It's heavier than I thought it would be," Jason called, and the three of them turned to their left, now facing east, and ran down to the corner. They then turned south and kicked open the door that lead into the north corridor. Kara ran in first, then Sullivan, and finally Jason, who turned and closed the door behind them. He turned and saw a cluttered, small back corridor with grey walls and rows of shelves that held cardboard boxes and cleaning supplies for the maintenance crew. He followed Kara and Sullivan, who were patiently waiting for him, down the corridor and out the other door, entering the east wing of the building. As they looked around, they spotted more zombies, but the shambling figures hadn't noticed them yet. The three of them then crept along the wall, staying out of the zombies' sight as much as possible and heading to the east.

"Where are we going?" asked Kara, and Jason turned and shrugged. She rolled her eyes at him and looked down at Sullivan, who smiled up at her and gave a little whimper.

"You don't know where to go either, do you?" she asked, and he gave a little pant before licking his lips. She smirked and shook her head at him, running into Jason's back and nearly pushing them both over.

"What?" she barked as quietly as possible at him. He turned to face her with a grim expression.

"He's right, you know—we're going to need food if we're locked up in this building. And I've seen zombie movies before. Other people want food too. Violent people, most of the time," he said in a low voice.

"Locked up in here? Like for months? No way. That can't be. The govern—"

"Will do what? They'll write this place off and nuke it rather than let the zombie apocalypse out," he snapped back at her, and he saw her skin go pale. Whatever hopes of escaping they may have had were gone.

"Okay, I lost it there for a bit. So what's the plan?" she asked, and he gulped.

"I need a gun," he said to her and continued to walk down the east wing, keeping close to the wall.

"You won't find one on this end. The guns are down at the other end of the mall, where we came from," she said, pulling a map out of her pocket.

"Where did you get that from?" he asked, and she raised her eye brows at him.

"They're in the pamphlets at the door of each end of this thing," she hissed, and he held up his hands in surrender.

"Well, we're screwed," Jason said, holding his head and falling against the wall. Kara walked over to him and knelt beside him.

"Don't give up on me. We need each other in this, whether we know each other or not. We might still be able to take the subway circuit back to the north wing if we hurry," she whispered to him, and he smiled at her. Sullivan ran over and licked his face before he stood up. The three continued until they came across the subway station. They were about to board when they heard clapping, and out came an African American man wearing a short-sleeved black tuxedo with a black bow, a grey undershirt, and dark mirror shades.

"Jax Caupo, one of the—"

"Higher-ups of OnLast—yeah, I've heard of you. In fact, there probably aren't many people who don't know who you are. What with all the posters, interviews, and commercials you've been in, how couldn't I know who you are?" Jason replied coldly.

"OnLast is the company who designed and funded Cosmic City, isn't it?" Kara asked.

"Yeah. 'Building a better future' is their motto," Jason answered, and Jax laughed.

"I'm very flattered. Now on to business. I figure that you might be in need of a gun?" Jax asked, shocking Jason and Kara. Sullivan made a grunt and turned his head to the side, staring cautiously at Jax.

"How did you know?" Jason asked in shock, and Jax smiled.

"Everyone needs a gun in these times. So is it a deal?" he replied, slipping a gun out of his sleeve like a magic trick.

"What do you want for it?" Jason asked warily and Jax's gaze drifted over to Kara.

"I want a good look at her," he said sinisterly, and Kara crossed her arms over her chest, scoffing at him.

"No way. Not a chance, buddy!" Jason barked and stepped in front of her. Jax frowned and shot him a dry look.

"Not a nude one. This isn't a porno, ya know?" Jax replied, cracking his neck. "I just want a look at Miss Hal—"

"Don't mention that name!" Kara snapped,

stepping out from behind Jason. Jason and Sullivan both stared at her in surprise.

"Okay, you win," she grumbled walking up to him. Sullivan gave a little whimper as he watched her walk up to Jax, perhaps wondering what was going to happen next. Jason tensed up like he was expecting a fight or something. Jax smirked and reached his hand down, wrapping his thumb and index finger around her chin and lifting her face up to get a good look. She just bit her lip and glared, letting him have his fun. If looks could kill, Jax's face would have rotted off. He smiled wider, showing his teeth, and then let go of her, throwing the gun toward Jason. Jason reached forward and fumbled to grab it, finally catching the gun by the barrel.

"It's an FN-57 and should be a good fit for you," Jax said before boarding the small bullet train that pulled up and came to a stop behind him.

"Why did you do this?" Jason asked, and Jax raised his arms, almost as if to showcase himself.

"What do men do with power?" he asked back to no answer. "Anything they want. This amused me, so I did it. And also you needed a gun if you're going to survive this event that I started," Jax finished, laughing as the train took off. Jason called out to him, having more questions, but there was no answer.

Kara walked slowly over to Jason, still hugging herself and trying to fight the creepy chill crawling up her spine.

"Are you okay?" Jason asked, and she nodded.

"Let's just go," she said, and the three turned and headed off to the west, going to find a safe place to bunker down. Jason spit out his gum and stuck his gun in the back of his pants, feeling like a street gangster now.

"You're going to need target practice," Kara said after a moment of silence.

"Yep," Jason said, smirking back at her.

3. THE GARDENS

3. THE GARDENS

Gardens are all very different and as varied as the plants that are in them. What most people don't think about, though, is what lurks in them.

J ason checked the ammo in his new handgun, seeing if the small pain they had gone through for it was worth it, and sure enough, there were a full 20 rounds in the clip. He smiled and slid the clip back into his gun, feeling already like a pro. His father had been in the military, and his brother had been a gun enthusiast, so he knew a bit about his guns and which guns were which.

"So?" asked Kara as she looked down at it. He turned and nodded at her, his hands shaking as he waited for the chance to fire it.

"It's good," he said, turning his attention to the fumbling zombie only about 15 feet away from them.

They had managed to find an isolated zombie, and for whatever reason, it hadn't noticed them yet. Jason took a deep breath, holding his arm out and pointing the gun at the zombie. This was his first time firing the gun, let alone firing at a moving, somewhat living thing. He took another deep breath and then squeezed the trigger three times. The first shot hit the shop window to the right of the zombie, the second hit the stand far behind the zombie, and the last nicked the thing's hand. Kara stood in shock as she watched with a dumbfounded expression. Not only had he totally missed all three, but the zombie hadn't even noticed. Had they found the dumbest zombie out there? Jason just stood still, his eye twitching, dumbfounded by his aim. He shook his head and then took aim again. As he did, Sullivan laid down beside Kara, watching with wonder. Jason fired another two shots, missing the first again but hitting the zombie in the arm with his second shot. He smiled and turned to Kara, who gave him a look of appreciation. Their celebration was cut short by a loud growl. They turned to see the zombie that Jason had shot charging them with surprising speed. Sullivan barked and jumped up, running over and grabbing the thing by its ankle, yanking it to the ground. It rolled and wriggled, but Jason hurried over and kicked it over, aiming the gun carefully at its head and pulling the trigger. It stopped moving. Jason looked down at Sullivan and rubbed his head, feeding him a treat he had taken from the convenience store. He then counted his shots and figured he had about 14 more bullets.

"We need to head to the gun store now," he said as he faced Kara.

"What for? We have a gun," she replied, staring into his eyes as if looking for an answer. He smiled and walked over to her.

"We are going to run out of ammo and need more than this," he said, showing her how many shots he had left. She nodded slowly, understanding now.

"Okay, let's go, but with your accuracy we should try shooting as little as possible," she said, and he nodded in response. The two then turned and began heading northwest—with Sullivan trailing behind them—using her map as a guide and for general direction. They rushed out the door ahead of them and found themselves in a wide-open courtyard filled with lush, beautiful plants and tall, low-hanging trees. They looked around at the beautiful gardens that grew elegantly and naturally around three separate fountains and many sprinkler systems that meshed perfectly with the nature around them. Jason walked slowly down the stone path, stopping when he came across a hill of sandstone that formed a small, makeshift mountain with a cave entrance just up the trail.

"No way," Kara muttered as she walked up to him.

"Way," Jason replied as they stared up at it. A loud gurgling grabbed their attention, and they turned to find more zombies shambling toward them. Jason swung around and grabbed Kara's wrist, running with her up the northern path and zigzagging through the many bushes that lined it. Jason stopped at the door and kicked it open. He went in first and let Sullivan and Kara in behind him, shutting and locking the door behind as they entered. Jason turned around and saw that they were in the main shopping district, just the place they wanted to go.

"Now the gun store is up that escalator," Kara said, pointing toward a tall set of stairs.

"It's out of commission, isn't it?" Jason whined as they walked up to it. Kara nodded, and he shook his head, starting his long ascent up the stairs with Kara and Sullivan behind him. They made it up to the second floor a few long moments later, nearly winded by the amount of running they had been doing recently.

"We're here," Jason panted, pointing at the store on their right. The two walked over to the glass windows of the store and began window shopping. Jason took note of the incredibly large woman sitting on the slowly buckling office chair at the centre of the room. He would have placed her at 400 pounds by the way she looked, and she was no taller than five and a half feet. She snorted herself awake and raised her double-barrelled shotgun, firing a shot off at Jason and Kara. They ducked and hid behind the white counter for cover, the window shattering and raining glass onto them. Kara nearly let out a scream as she held her head. This was the first time either of them had been shot at.

"You think you can steal some of my guns?" the fat woman called, laughing. She had a distinctly redneck accent that Jason figured matched the cliché of a gun-shop owner.

"Don't shoot! We just need a place to—" Jason began to say as he slowly stood up, only to fall back down as she shot again. He pulled his gun out and took a deep breath.

"Are you going to shoot her?" Kara asked, and he shrugged.

"I … may have to," he drawled, cocking his gun.

"Jason, you are not a murderer," she said, trying to convince him to leave. But he shook his head, knowing that the gun he had was going to be their only real protection, and with his aim, they would need more ammo.

"It's self-defense," he said, and she frowned. "Besides, I'll try talking my way out first," he finished and heard the woman pumping her shotgun as she finished reloading.

"I know that you know you don't want to hurt us!" Jason called out to her.

"Are you trying to confuse me?" she asked and fired again, blowing a hole in their cover and forcing them to bounce to another counter. "Because I'm smarter than that."

Jason sighed and then peeked out at her. "Look," he began, "you know that we know that. And we know that we need in for some ammo just like you know we aren't evil." She turned, and he thought she was going to shoot, but she didn't. He stood up slowly with his hands up, and she looked at him. She smirked, and he jumped behind cover as she fired her gun again, blowing away more of the store.

"I knew that you thought I knew you were good, but you should've known that I know that you're evil. So you thought you knew that I knew but didn't because you're not!" she called, her face turning red as she laughed.

"What does that even mean?" Jason grumbled and

then jumped up when he heard the click of her gun, thinking she was trying to reload. But he saw right away that he was wrong about the click and had no idea where it had come from. She took aim one last time and pulled the trigger, only to get a click from her empty gun. Jason took aim, and as he fired, her chair gave way and the base exploded. She fell and cracked her head against the corner of the counter next to her. Jason's shot missed her and hit the mirror behind her. Kara stood up and looked at Jason, who was slowly approaching the woman. Sullivan, who had been hiding as instructed, ran into the store and began checking the place out. Jason walked over, gun raised, to the woman. A trail of blood had begun trickling from the side of her head, and she wasn't moving.

"She's dead," he muttered, going pale. Kara walked in and placed a hand on his shoulder, giving him a gentle squeeze to show she was there for him. He closed his eyes, shook his head, and then turned and looked around.

"We should start looking. Zombies are going to be here soon. The ammo should be behind the desk," he instructed her, and she quickly moved behind the front counter. As she did, he headed over to a nearly empty rack and picked up one of the guns, identifying it as a Mossberg 590 pump-action shotgun with an extended barrel. He snapped it open and figured it would hold about eight shots, unusual for a civilian model, he figured.

"Found them!" Kara called as she popped up from behind the counter, stopping when she saw him holding the gun.

"It looks good on you," she said, walking over to him and handing him two more clips for his handgun. "Are these the right ones?"

"Yeah, and I need some shells for this too, if there are any," he said to her as he pocketed the clips. She ducked behind the counter and then dug out every shotgun-shell box the store had. He smiled and walked over, sifting through the boxes until he came across the one he needed.

"Thank you," he said as she walked over to him. He loaded the gun and pumped the handle, readying it to fire. As he did, a zombie came shambling into the store, staring at Sullivan, who backed up and barked at it. Jason called to Sullivan to stay back, and as he did, the zombie noticed him and turned. Jason smiled and braced the stock against his shoulder, pulling the trigger. The gun went off and blew a wide hole through the zombie's head, throwing it over and onto its back. It wriggled and then went stiff on the floor.

"Yes, I love this gun!" Jason laughed, staring at it

like a kid with a new toy. Sullivan barked, and the two turned to see a pack of zombies charging them from across the store.

"Run!" Kara called, and Jason pocketed as many shells as he could and ran with her. There were far too many to shoot, but Jason tried anyway, turning and shooting his new gun. He took down two and was satisfied and then turned and caught up to Kara. The three ran down the hall and to the escalator, darting down it and back down the shopping district and heading for the gardens. Kara unlocked the door and let Jason and Sullivan out, this time taking her turn to follow them out and bar the door. They stopped and turned around; the zombies they had left there were still shambling around throughout the gardens. Jason passed his handgun to Kara and gestured to her to be silent. She stared uncomfortably at the gun and then looked up at him. He nodded to her, and the three of them stole through the almost forest-like gardens, making their way to the mouth of the cave at the peak of the sandstone mountain.

"Ready?" Jason asked her as they stared into the shimmering cave. She nodded and turned to him.

"You first," she said, and he shook his head, entering the cave with Sullivan beside him. Kara gripped the gun and followed after him.

4. REAPER'S TOLL

4. REAPER'S TOLL

We all live for the same thing—to die. People live to die and die to live again. But who's going to pay the reaper's toll first?

Lights danced across the stone walls of the cave as the two walked down the widening passageway using flashlights that they had found near the mouth of the cave to light their way. Kara looked cautiously around, noting how the walls shimmered as if there was a large body of water around them, but the caves looked dry. She crashed into Jason's back when he suddenly came to a stop.

"What?" she grumbled, rubbing her head. She looked past him and saw that the cave forked up ahead, one path leading straight on and the other leading down into pitch-black darkness.

"Which way?" Jason grumbled, looking around and clenching his shotgun. Something seemed off to him, like there was someone stalking them and eyeing them from the darkness. He couldn't shake the feeling and could barely ignore the cold chill that crawled its way down his spine. He began to wonder if Kara could feel it too and looked down at her. She was looking back and forth between the passageways, but he had a pretty good guess which one she wanted by the look in her eyes.

Sullivan turned and began to yip at the dark passageway, and Jason took that as a sign to go the other way.

"It looks like we're all feeling it then?" Jason asked, and Kara gulped. She stood in silence for another short moment and then turned to face him.

"Let's go. I don't want to dawdle here much longer," she said finally, and Jason nodded. The two of them turned and headed down the path ahead of them, turning and calling Sullivan. His ears perked up, and he came running along beside them, his hackles still standing slightly on end. The three of them walked cautiously through the tunnels, turning and following the snaking path, unsure of what they would find. Moments later, they came across a clearing like a cave within a cave that was illuminated by a light shining from above. Kara stared up at the light, thinking it was from the mall above but that it was rather bright. As she stared up, Jason looked down along the spiraling stone path that clung to the walls and led down to a pond below.

"Is this where the shimmering walls came from?" Kara asked as she began to follow Jason down the path.

"No, we were too far away … I don't know what that effect was from." Jason shook his head, staring cautiously down the pathway. The cave so far had been surprisingly quiet and never seemed to have a single zombie lurking within it. Jason sighed in relief but knew deep inside that it probably wasn't a good thing. *What could scare a zombie?* he thought as they turned down another passage near the edge of the underground pond. As they turned their first corner, they were suddenly struck by a shockwave of air that blew their hair around. Jason looked down, and their flashlights had been fried.

"What was that?" he asked, raising his shotgun and aiming it down the tunnels. The path had grown dark, with only a green glow barely illuminating the cave. Kara raised her handgun and pointed it down the same tunnel Jason was facing. Sullivan went into a low stance as his fur spiked up, and he began to bark and growl. Jason then could have sworn that he heard a hissing noise, and he narrowed his eyes as he tried to see into the dark. And it was then that he saw what looked like a shadow within a shadow.

"What is it?" he murmured, tightening his grip on his gun. A tall, slender figure wearing long, flowing black clothes came out of the shadows wearing a hood and mask over its face that revealed only its glowing red eyes. Jason felt a cold chill hit him as he saw it almost gliding across the ground, moving swiftly but menacingly toward them. Jason opened fire, blasting the creature with his shotgun as many times as he could. But there was no effect, and the creature never slowed at all.

"Run!" Jason called, turning and darting back down the cave with Kara and Sullivan. The creature dropped a long chain out of its sleeve, masterfully swinging and throwing it at Jason, catching his leg and tripping him onto the floor.

"Jason!" Kara screamed as it began pulling him toward it. Jason yelled as he tried to grip something but couldn't find anything to grab as he got ever closer to the creature. He managed to roll around and aim his shotgun at the creature again. It gave a huge tug as he fired, causing him to miss and hit the roof. The stones above cracked and began to split, letting rays of light into the cave. The light hit the creature, and it dropped the chain, letting out a blood-chilling howl as it began to turn into burning ash. Jason watched in shock as it turned into a pile of white, burning dust and then vanished. Kara ran over to Jason and helped him to his feet.

"Are you okay? What was that thing?" she asked frantically.

"Yeah, I'm fine, I think … I don't know what it was, but we should go before more come," Jason replied, filling his shotgun with more shells. Whatever it was, it wasn't a zombie, and Jason didn't want to stay and see if it had friends. The three of them darted back down the path and through the twisting hallways, making haste this time. They stopped when they came across a dead end with a perfectly shaped wooden board stuck in the stone wall. Jason stared curiously at it as Kara crawled up the small pile of stones and reached out for the wooden board. He then looked down slightly and let his eyes linger on Kara, his thoughts slowly drifting as his eyes travelled down her. As he stared, Kara began feeling out the wooden board, stopping when she pushed on it and it collapsed, revealing a closet on the other side.

"We're in!" she called, and Jason shook his head, following her through the closet and into the small apartment room.

"The caves lead to a room? Cool," Jason mumbled,

looking around. He felt a cold chill trace his back and turned sharply, hearing a hissing noise coming from the cave in the closet. He raised the board and blocked the cave off and then closed the closet doors and barred them shut with a nearby broom.

"Let's go to another room?" Jason suggested, and Kara agreed, finding it too creepy to stay in that room. They left the apartment and walked down the hallway, counting the room numbers as they went.

"How about this one?" Jason said, opening the room at the end of the hall. Past the doorway was the most luxurious apartment in the building, with its own fireplace, piano, and minibar. Kara walked in first, looking slowly around. The room was warmly painted a creamy beige with oak finishing, with a door on the left side of the room that led to a good-sized bathroom and shower.

"Okay," she said in a daze. Her family had never been rich and would *never* have had a chance to rent this room in her lifetime. Jason smiled, folding up the map he slipped from her pocket and tucking it away. If things were going to hell, he was going to take advantage and live in style. He looked around and saw no sign of danger or of this room's past residents. The door wasn't locked, so he figured that maybe the door had been damaged in the outbreak.

"Finally I can have a shower," Kara moaned, walking into the bathroom. Jason leaned against the couch and stared at the open bathroom door. His thoughts trailed off as he began to reflect on everything that had happened. He took a deep breath, finally feeling like he had the chance to mourn his brother's death. A lot had happened to him lately, and it had only been a few hours. Jason continued gazing through the bathroom door, staring off in space until Kara caught his eye as she was bending over and dropping her slightly dust-coated jeans to her ankles. He smiled and continued to watch, his thoughts turning in a different direction. He pivoted slightly toward the door, and as he did, she spotted him staring. She gasped and grabbed the weight scale, chucking it at his face, missing her mark when he ducked suddenly. She slammed the door closed, and he heard a gun cocking.

"You're a pervert! If I catch you again, I'm going to shoot you!" she screamed through the door. Jason could tell she was serious about shooting him. He fell against the back of the couch and stared up at the fan that was rotating slowly. He felt like trying to explain that he wasn't really looking but knew she wouldn't believe him anyway. *Pervert? I'm not a pervert!* He cursed in his head as he walked over and fell back on the couch. He stretched out and closed his eyes.

❖　　❖　　❖

Kara wrapped herself in a towel and approached the shower. It had occurred to her that the water might not even work, but she figured she'd try anyway. She reached in and twisted the knob, and it squeaked a little. Nothing happened at first, but then the water came bursting out of the shower head. She sighed in relief and climbed in. She then paused suddenly as everything that had happened recently began to pour over her like the water from the shower head. She caught herself on the tile walls and hung her head low. She had been in shock and in survival mode for what seemed like so long that when she finally had a chance to relax, to let her guard down, it just all hit her at once. Crazed people trying to shoot them, hordes of disgusting, rot-infested zombies trying to eat them, and Sam's death were all too much for her. Sam had been the only person who had kept care of her while she was living on the streets. He had been like a brother to her, and in an instant, he was gone and she had been in too much shock to have given it any thought. She noticed her hands trembling and held them. Then she stood up straight and took another deep breath. Jason appeared in her mind with his black hair, silver-blue eyes, and unwavering expression. She smiled inside at that thought …

⬦ ⬦ ⬦

Jason smiled when he heard the water come on. It meant that the government hadn't cut off the water yet. He took the chance to stroll over to the kitchen that was built into the room and turn on the tap. He bent over the counter and began slurping the cold, refreshing water. Sullivan whimpered, and he looked down at him. Jason stopped drinking and filled a bowl of water and set it on the floor for Sullivan to drink from. He then opened the small refrigerator and pulled out a wrapped-up ham sandwich, unwrapped it, and took a big bite.

"I can finally eat!" He moaned the same way Kara had and took another bite. He fed the last of it to Sullivan and began pulling more food out of the fridge. He set the food down onto the island in the centre of the kitchen, and as he did, Kara came walking out of the bathroom wearing a towel. This was the first time he had seen her long, raven hair out of a ponytail. Her hair draped down and covered her shoulders, going all the way down to the middle of her back.

"You found food?" she said, blinking at the sight

of the food-covered table. Jason stared at her wet shoulders and legs, and she scoffed.

"Do you want me to shoot you?" she hissed, and he waved his hands in front of himself, shaking his head.

"No! I was … um … just waiting food for … ready," he said quickly back to her. *Stupid! That sounded utterly retarded. What's wrong with me?* he thought to himself as she smirked wryly at him. She walked back to the bathroom to get dressed, taking one of the nightgowns from the closet near the bathroom door. Jason slapped his forehead and sighed, shaking his head. He then fell back on his chair and shoved his fork into his mashed potatoes. He took a bite of them, not caring that they were cold; he felt like he hadn't eaten for ages. Kara walked back out wearing a sand-coloured, knee-length nightgown with her hair tied back up in a ponytail.

"It all looks so good," she drawled, reaching over and breaking apart some Italian bread. They dined until they couldn't eat anymore, throwing down some table scraps for Sullivan every so often. After they finished eating, Jason walked his way over to the light and flicked it off and then made himself a bed on the floor beside the large, queen-size bed that he gave to Kara and Sullivan.

Almost two hours passed, and Jason still lay awake

with his fingers linked behind his head for support. He could tell that Kara wasn't asleep either. The sound of her breathing, or the lack of it, indicated that she was wide awake. He glanced over at the bed, sensing her eyes on him. He wasn't sure, but it almost seemed like Kara's eyes glowed in the dark. Instead of scaring him, it made him feel oddly invulnerable.

5. Sniper

They say that the best weapon is one you only have to fire once. But for me, the best weapon is the one that's never been fired.

Jason's eyes snapped open as he sat up, woken by the sound of a loud explosion somewhere near them. Kara and Sullivan had been startled awake by it too.

"What was that?" Jason asked, holding his throbbing head. He never had been good with being woken up by loud noises. Kara jumped out of bed and dragged Jason to his feet. He stretched and cracked his back, then moved swiftly over to his backpack and shotgun, taking a moment to toss Kara her handgun. She grabbed her stuff as well, slinging the fire axe over her shoulder and checking her gun as Sullivan barked at the door.

Jason figured that meant it was time to go and opened the door. A heavy zombie fell through it on top of him, pinning him to the floor. He struggled as he tried to fight it off, jerking his head to the side to avoid a deadly chomp to the face. Sullivan grabbed it by the neck and dragged it off of Jason, allowing him time to roll away. Sullivan struggled with the zombie as it began to fight back until Kara came over and swung the fire axe in a long arc, beheading the ghoul before it could bite their dog.

"That's why you were barking," Jason mused between deep breaths as he rubbed Sullivan's head. Kara then called to him, and the three of them ran out the door, only to find themselves surrounded in the hallway by half a dozen zombies.

"The sound came from somewhere on the main floor. Should we check it out?" Kara asked, taking a swing with her axe and decapitating a zombie. Jason bashed one of the zombies away with the butt of his gun, taking a moment to pause and think about it.

"The sound will have attracted a lot of these things, but … I want to find out what it was, so I guess we're going that way," he said as he ran and pushed the zombies aside, Kara following right behind him. The three of them fought their way past the oncoming waves of corpses and kicked down the door to the emergency staircase. Jason led them down a couple of flights of stairs, making it safely to the main floor. He checked the window to make sure it was clear before pushing the door open and letting his friends out; then he closed it off and, with Kara's help, knocked over a vending machine to block the zombies out.

"Now which way?" Jason asked as he looked around. Kara gripped his shoulder to grab his attention and pointed toward a cloud of smoke creeping across the glass roof just west of them.

"Oh," he mumbled and began walking toward the smoke. Kara followed and kept a sharp eye out for zombies. The loud noise had to have attracted at least a small swarm of them, and she didn't want to be caught in the stampede, mauled, and ripped apart because of their curiosity.

Curiosity killed the cat, she thought as the three carefully proceeded down the west wing past some bloodied kiosks and over some spilled gumballs. They stopped when they arrived at a partially destroyed Yukatan casino. The smoke was pouring out of the destroyed roof, and an entire wall had been blown outward. Small flames were still creeping out of the destroyed section of the wall. Jason and Kara walked over, stepping over the debris and into the casino. Their attention was immediately grabbed by the flaming wreckage of a Blackhawk helicopter. Jason could tell the design had been changed slightly, making it somewhat narrower and giving it small wings that held rocket pods. He figured it looked like some kind of stealth assault chopper that the military might have developed.

"Sweet," he couldn't help himself from saying.

"What is a military attack chopper doing here? And how did it get destroyed?" Kara asked as she cautiously approached the wreckage. Jason looked up and saw a section of the roof that looked as though the helicopter had blown through it with its missiles. He continued scanning the roof and saw a destroyed section of catwalk above them and a shattered section of wall.

"I've seen enough action movies to know what happened here," he concluded, moving swiftly over to Kara. He stepped over the sharp, shredded steel and began checking out the interior. The flames were hot, and the thought of it exploding on him drifted through his mind, but that wouldn't stop him from scavenging for supplies. He called Kara over to help him pull out a thick steel crate that was trapped by some twisted metal. They both grabbed on and pulled hard, falling out of the chopper as the crate came loose from the wreckage. Jason sat up and laughed, walked over, knelt down in front of the crate, and then cursed as he lifted a thick steel lock. Kara came down hard on the lock with her ax, chopping it in two and sending the pieces flying. He pulled his hand away quickly, glaring at her with wide eyes.

"Were you trying to slice my fingers off?" he barked.

"I knew you would move," she mumbled back to him and pried the crate open.

"Wow," the two drawled as they stared in. Resting neatly in the crate was a sniper rifle with three small boxes of ammunition. At first blush, someone could have mistaken it for an US Marine Corps M40A5 sniper. But Jason could tell it was a modified version of some other gun using the A5 as a base. Jason picked the gun up. It was heavier than he had thought it would be. The rifle had an under-barrel tripod and an adjustable scope along with a 15-bullet cartridge. Sullivan's barking caught their attention, and they turned to see the oncoming wave of zombies that they had feared would come. Kara turned back to Jason, and he passed her the sniper and shoved the ammunition into her backpack.

"You don't want it?" she asked, and he raised his shotgun.

"Nah, I prefer a close-up punch and being the centre of attention," he replied with a smirk, and the two ran out of the casino. Jason pumped his gun and turned sharply, blasting a hole through a ghoul's head and throwing its motionless body into a stack of other oncoming zombies. Jason pumped again and turned to fire. His breath halted when he heard the dreaded click. No ammo. He screamed and jumped back, using his gun to push away the zombie before it could tackle him. Kara pulled out her handgun and shot it in the temple, killing it with a single shot. He never had time to say thank you, as more came. The two turned and, with Sullivan beside them, ran down the west wing heading east. They came across an out-of-order escalator and began dashing up it, knocking over luggage and ornaments, doing anything they could to slow their pursuers. The zombies tripped on the luggage and the stairs, falling over and toppling the other zombies that tried to make their way up behind those in the front. The three of them made it to the top, and Jason turned to see if they were followed. The zombies were still falling over each other and began to form a dog pile. Jason shook his head at their stupidity and turned to face Kara again, figuring that the zombies wouldn't be able to make it up to get them in this lifetime. Before anything else could happen, Jason reached in his pockets and pulled out the shotgun shells Kara had grabbed for him and began reloading his gun. He then walked over to the other side and leaned over the protection rails, taking a look at the mall below them just down another flight of steps. He spotted something off in the distance and narrowed his eyes, trying to get a better look at it.

"Look at that." He whistled, and Kara walked over.

"Oh my god!" Kara whispered under her breath. What they were staring at was an abandoned armoured military Hummer with a narrow, box-like design and a mounted .50-calibre machinegun.

"That's an attractive-looking vehicle," she said, nearly drooling.

"I didn't know you were into vehicles," Jason remarked, and she shot a grin at him.

"Not all vehicles, just tank-like jeeps like that one."

"Oh, okay," Jason replied as he finished loading his shotgun.

"So, what's the—"

"You cover me with that sniper rifle, and I'll go get it, bring it around, and you can jump in," Jason said quickly in the middle of her sentence.

"Can you drive?" she asked, and he began down the steps.

"Can you shoot?" he replied rhetorically, and she gave him a dry smirk. Jason couldn't drive anything beyond a golf cart, but he figured he had to learn some time, and what a way to learn! Jason began pushing his way through the crowd of zombies, knocking some over on his way through. He heard a couple of loud shots come from behind. None of the zombies went down.

"How do I do this?" Kara called down at him.

"Use the force!" Jason called back, blasting back a wave of ghouls with a shot from his gun. He heard another shot and then another, and finally a zombie's head exploded like a watermelon. He covered his face and choked a little. Not even his shotgun could do that. He then turned and—with Kara covering him—made a dash toward the Hummer. He jumped and slid across the slightly dented hood and jumped into the open driver's seat, slamming the door on his way in. He looked to his side and saw a military machete in a leather sheath. He reached over and lifted it up, setting it on his lap.

"Kara can keep the axe." He chuckled and looked around.

Kara fired another two shots and cursed under her breath.

"Where is he?" she mumbled, watching the Hummer with her scope. The vehicle then roared to life and awkwardly backed up, smashing into some decorative stands behind it. She laughed a little, and the jeep turned and began to accelerate toward her. It stopped and twisted to its side, and she jumped on the roof, followed closely by Sullivan, and climbed down through the hole where the gunner would stand.

"You drive," Jason said to her and shifted out of the seat. She sat down and got a feel for the controls. As she did, Jason climbed up and took hold of the mounted gun.

"Head toward the central courtyard!" he called down to her, and she sped forward, running down some oncoming zombies as she raced toward the large doors that led into the northwest courtyard. Jason gripped the trigger on the gun, letting out a barrage of bullets that shredded the door to pieces. The vibrations from the gun shook him as he continued to squeeze the trigger and tear apart the zombies ahead of them. The Hummer came crashing out of the now-open doorway and skidded to a halt on the marble checkered floor tiles that made a path to the fountain in the middle of the courtyard. Jason sat down, his whole body still vibrating, and took a deep breath. He reached over and petted Sullivan, who had been along for the whole ride.

"Look, Jason, the SPU bunker is just ahead," Kara said, and he leaned over the front seat to look through the windshield.

"That's the special protection unit, right?" he asked, and she nodded.

"Sounds good," he said, and she stepped on the gas pedal.

6. SPU

The truth is covered in shadow, and lies shine brightly in the spotlight. Our world is so twisted that we've become okay with that and have accepted it.

The ride had been for the most part smooth, with a few bumps from annoying potholes cropping up every so often. Jason braced himself as the Hummer came crashing through the east entrance doors and slid to a grinding halt. Jason and Kara looked slowly around the area, scanning carefully for zombies. But beyond a few stragglers, there weren't any. Jason had thought at first that he would feel relieved, but he didn't. There should have been a couple dozen based only on the crowd of tourists he had seen upon first arriving at Cosmic City. And he had seen enough zombie flicks to know zombies didn't just disappear. At first he had thought it was the military, having found the downed helicopter and abandoned military jeep. But the way that they had found them gnawed at his gut: abandoned and destroyed, not to mention that they hadn't actually encountered any military personnel so far. There was no way that the military had control of the situation.

The Hummer drove down the east wing and stopped at a service elevator marked SPU. Jason jumped out first and began waltzing toward the elevator.

"Hold on," Kara called, stepping out of the Hummer.

"What's up, Kara?" Jason called back.

"You don't find anything strange about this? That the government decided to build a survival bunker in a mall or that there aren't any SPU personnel to check us over?" she replied, crossing her arms over her chest and looking around cautiously.

"I hadn't thought of it that way, but it's our only chance of finding supplies or any more clues to the mystery, so ..." Jason replied, pushing the button to call the elevator up to them. Kara rolled her eyes at him as he smirked. The elevator opened, and out shambled a half a dozen zombies. Jason jumped away from the elevator and took aim with his shotgun. The two opened fire, expertly killing off the clumped-up crowd of corpses. Jason checked his gun and then mumbled under his breath.

"What's wrong?" Kara asked.

"I'm out of ammo. Let's hope we find some in there," he replied, and she began digging in her pockets. Jason watched as she extended her hand and revealed three shotgun shells. He looked stunned for a moment and then smiled back at her and took them. They lingered for a moment and then quickly retracted their hands from one another. With a bark from Sullivan, the three entered the elevator, unsure of what they would find.

The elevator dinged, and the thick doors slid open. Inside, the bunker looked as if it had been ransacked. A lightbulb swung from the roof; crates had been dumped over and shelves destroyed. Jason looked around. There was nothing … except for plenty of blood smearing the walls and painting the floor. Kara couldn't help but cover her mouth with her hands as she glanced at the gore around her.

"There's nothing—nothing at all!" Jason cursed as he tossed a crate aside. He had checked through ammo boxes and food crates, looking for any supplies. He rubbed his face with his hands and stared up at the wall. He then stood up quickly as he spotted something he hadn't seen on his first search through the room. Words had been carved into the thick walls.

"Nice try, little piggy," Jason said as he read the words out loud.

"What was that?" Kara snapped at him.

"No, the words on the wall," Jason replied, and Kara walked over. Kara then spotted the monitors and sat down in front of them. She began typing on the keyboard.

"What are you doing?" Jason asked as one of the monitors started bringing up a file directory.

"I'm checking the SPU's files for any useful information they might have had," she replied, and Jason nodded approvingly like the proud boss of an attractive secretary. Jason shook the thoughts from his head and watched as some locked files started popping open.

"All this and you can hack too?" Jason commented as the files were successfully decoded. She gave him a wry smirk and continued reading.

"It's saying something about Project Z. And a sacred cave … or something similar to that," Kara stumbled as she tried to read through the ancient Greek dialect that the SPU had used to code their files and keep them safe.

"So the building of this bunker in a shopping mall and how quickly the military reacted to the situation was no accident?" Jason asked half-sarcastically. She shot him a dry look and then kept on reading.

"Jason, the cave is under Cosmic City. That's why this was built here—to cover it up!" Kara concluded.

"Wait, there's a cave entrance in the northeast gardens!" Jason replied, raising a finger in an aha gesture. He then lifted his gun up and began walking toward the elevator.

"Wait, Jason—look!" Kara called, and Jason ran over. He looked through the security monitor and saw a line of armed soldiers aiming their guns at the elevator.

"They know we're in here," Kara mumbled, and Jason looked past the monitors and into the darkest corner of the room. He then raised Kara's handgun and shot the small camera that had been spying on them.

"Well, this is great. Now what?" Kara cursed as Jason placed his fist on his chin and began to pace.

"I've got it!" he said finally, walking over and pushing the Up button of the elevator and stepping out.

"What are you doing?" Kara asked, walking over to him. The elevator stopped, and its ding was followed by a loud barrage of gunfire. The soldiers unloaded half a clip of ammo each as the elevator doors slid open, halting their fire finally after they found no one in the elevator.

"Was the info wrong?" Jason heard one of them ask.

He didn't get a reply. The soldiers boarded the elevator, and Jason told Kara to take cover behind the walls and out of sight of the soldiers. When the elevator dinged, Jason and Kara stuck their guns into the elevator while keeping in cover, and began pulling their triggers. After a short pause, Jason and Kara felt brave enough and stuck their heads around the corner. The soldiers were all dead and slumped against the back of the service elevator, their blood pooling on the elevator floor. Jason stepped in first and picked up one of their black SCAR-H assault rifles, checking the mag and the barrel and stocking up on ammo clips. He then passed Kara more ammo for her handgun. The three of them boarded the elevator and pushed the Up button. The elevator shook all the way up, causing tension at the thought that it could fall, but that tension was relieved when it finally dinged at the main floor and they all came piling out like the zombies had done before them. They took a quick look around for any more hostile personnel before boarding their Hummer.

"Wait. Before we go, I have to know something," Jason said, placing his hand on Kara's shoulder.

"I can read ancient Egyptian too, and—"

"Jason, it was Greek," she corrected him, and he waved her off. He never had been any good at remembering names.

"The point is that I understood some of it, and it mentioned your name. Now this is the second time that your name or your family's name has come up, and I want in on the secret!"

She shot him a look of pain and scorn. At first Jason would've backed down, but not this time. He had to know. Kara took a deep breath, and then finally answered.

"I don't really know myself. All I know is that I'm the daughter of some infamous treasure hunter and that he left me alone to fend for myself. I also have a brother out there who I know nothing about," she said in a strangled voice. Jason squeezed her shoulder to let her know he was there for her.

"Let's go," he said after a moment of rest, and she nodded in response. The Hummer roared to life once more and sped down the hallway to the northeast gardens, flying out the smashed doors and skidding to a halt by the cave entrance, crushing some zombies who had gotten in their way.

They stopped for a moment to stare at the dark, shimmering entrance, recalling the horror they had already faced in there. Jason had begun to call the creature that had attacked them the Reaper. He figured the name fit. Kara looked over at him.

"You all set?" she asked, and he checked his

shotgun, his assault rifle, and finally his machete. With a confident yet still slightly spooked smirk, he nodded, and they climbed out of the Hummer. He wished that they could've just driven it right into the cave, but the Hummer wouldn't even come close to fitting and would have gotten stuck or caused a cave-in. He saluted it before following Kara into the cave with Sullivan trailing behind them.

7. THE TRUTH

7. THE TRUTH

People often say that it's easy to conceal the truth. But even with shadows upon shadows within shadows, the truth always seems to show.

The caves seemed to go on for an eternity, twisting and turning like a well-crafted labyrinth. Jason took a deep breath, smelling the damp, underground air of the cave and wishing he was outside. But he knew he had to press on. Whatever was down here, according to what they had read on the SPU computer, was the whole reason behind the zombie outbreak, behind Cosmic City, and maybe even behind Kara's family history. If he turned back now, he knew he would never know and never be able to escape the undead that lurked both in and out of this cave. Jason closed his eyes and began rubbing his forehead. A lot had been on his mind lately. He hadn't gotten to mourn his brother's death, and he had just killed soldiers from the army. Soldiers like his father once had been.

"Are you all right, Jason?" Kara asked, placing a hand on his shoulder.

"Yeah, just dirt from the roof," he replied, raising his shotgun again. He held his breath and stepped around the next corner, unsure of what he might find. Again there was nothing. He breathed out and continued traversing the cave.

"Which way?" Jason asked as they came across a forked passageway. Kara placed her hand over her mouth as she looked down each passageway, unsure of the one that would lead the right way. She didn't even know what they were looking for, which made choosing a path much harder. Before she could voice her opinion, a loud explosion was heard from the left tunnel, causing the entire cave to violently shake. Thinking fast, Jason leapt over Kara and shielded her. After the shaking had ceased, Kara opened her eyes and stared into Jason's; his face was mere inches away from hers. Jason quickly pulled himself away and helped her to her feet. Jason then swiped his hand down his pants for a quick dust off and looked around. The leftmost passage had been caved in.

"Great, at least we get one less choice," he grumbled, shaking his head. "Come on. Let's go this way before it blows up too," he said after a brief moment of silence. Kara agreed and called Sullivan to her side. The three darted down the right passage, not taking as much time as they had last time. Jason turned the corner and skidded to a halt as he reached a large clearing. Kara came up behind him and gasped. A massive chamber sat in front of them, carved out of the cave and lit up by a hole in the roof that allowed light in. There were stone stairs just ahead of them that lead to an empty altar. Jason stepped out into the chamber, immediately spotting a massive drop on either side of the stone walkway that lead up to the stairs. He stared down into the darkness below and then continued walking toward the altar with Sullivan behind him. Jason then heard a scream from behind. He whipped around and saw a man with his arm wrapped around Kara's neck. For a moment, Jason wondered who the man was. But he soon recognized Snake, the man who had kidnapped Jason and Kara and killed his brother. Snake laughed sadistically, raising a hunting knife and resting the blade on Kara's cheek just under her right eye.

"Let her go!" Jason barked, and Sullivan began snarling, his hackles spiking up. Jason raised his shotgun and pumped it.

"What are you going to do, little pig, blast through your girlfriend to get to me?" Snake laughed, swaying her from side to side. Jason gritted his teeth and tossed his shotgun down.

"Now the rest of your weapons." Snake chuckled, nicking Kara's cheek with his knife.

"Don't do it, Jason!" Kara called, and Snake tightened his arm on her neck, strangling her.

"All right, you win," Jason replied, tossing his assault rifle and machete down onto the ground and kicking them off the edge. Snake laughed and pulled Kara's handgun out. Then he threw her into the cave wall beside him, knocking her unconscious.

"You thought you could escape from me, didn't you, little piggy?" Snake chuckled, walking toward Jason with his gun raised.

"Piggy … Wait, so you're the one who raided the SPU bunker?" Jason asked with venom in his breath.

"'Bout time you figured it out." Snake laughed. As he did, Sullivan barked and made a lunge for him. Snake aimed, and the gun went off. Jason charged. Snake punted Sullivan aside, and Jason punched him in the face and followed up with a knee to the gut. Jason then threw out a left hook, connecting with Snake's jaw. Jason stopped and stared at Snake with a perplexed look on his face as the man he was beating began to laugh like a maniac. Snake faced Jason again and raised his arms.

"I didn't even feel that, bro." Snake chuckled and then punched Jason across the face. Snake followed up with a knee to Jason's gut and then finally elbowed him in the back of the neck. Jason went to stand, and Snake punted him in the ribs, throwing him over onto his side. Jason held his ribs and rolled onto his back, gritting his teeth. Snake smiled and walked over, lifting Jason by his collar and throwing him toward the edge of the pathway. Jason skidded on his stomach toward the edge, catching himself on the stone ledge before he could fall all the way off. Snake then walked up to him and knelt down.

"You see this place, Jason?" Snake asked, grabbing a fistful of Jason's hair and making him look around the chamber.

"It's the truth you've been looking for." He chuckled, placing a foot on Jason's fingers.

"What are you talking about?" Jason snarled, and Snake made him look at his face. Jason saw the dark veins and the pale grey skin that he hadn't noticed in his fit of rage.

"You're one of them?" Jason said with a sharp breath, and Snake chuckled, raising his forearm so Jason could see it. Jason looked and saw a large, rotting gouge in his arm with the reek of decomposing flesh emanating from it.

"How?" Jason snarled as Snake put more pressure on his fingers, slowly crushing them.

"Fair question, and your last one," Snake replied. Then he released Jason's hair so he could point at his wristband, which had a brilliant green gem embedded in it. Snake stood up and turned around, pacing and finally coming to a stop at the bottom of the stone stairs that led up to the altar.

"It calls to me, you know? The whispers and the commands. It's in this room, you know. And we serve it. All of us ... The mask is guarded by this altar," Snake began to speak in short fragments. "I've even bitten someone. A man from the SPU. Mason ..." he murmured, and Jason began pulling himself up. Snake turned around, and Sullivan leapt at him, clamping down hard on his arm. Snake shook his arm and threw Sullivan to the ground. Then he aimed his gun at Sullivan. Before he could pull the trigger, Jason ran over and tackled him, throwing the two of them over the edge and into the dark abyss below.

❖   ❖   ❖

Sullivan stared down and began to bark. His barking stirred Kara, and she began to stand up, her vision blurry and her balance slightly off. She held her hand to her bleeding head and limped over to Sullivan, who began to howl.

"Jason!" Kara called a few times, glancing around the chamber, but she couldn't find him or Snake anywhere.

"Did he fall?" she asked herself, staring down into the darkness. Her thoughts were then grabbed by the howl that came from the cave followed swiftly by a sudden burst of wind. She knew what that meant and began to back away from the cave entrance with Sullivan. From the shadows came a reaper holding onto its long, thick chain and gliding across the floor toward her. It was followed by three others, all heading for her. She began backing up the stone steps, not letting her eyes off of them.

"Why are there so many?" she whispered in a strangled voice. It was as if they were taking the air from her. She tripped on the last step and caught herself on the altar with her bloody hand ...

✦   ✦   ✦

Jason opened his eyes and choked up some water. His whole body burned as if he had drowned. He turned around slowly and saw an underground river that led deeper into the cave. Jason figured the water must have broken his fall and he had washed up on these rocks. It occurred to him that the river probably wasn't deep enough to have broken his fall, but as long as he was alive, it didn't really matter to him. His thoughts then gathered, and he began looking around for Snake, who had fallen with him. But he saw no signs of him anywhere. He got to his feet and turned around, seeing a tunnel that led upward. He started to walk, but a green glow caught his attention. He turned to his right and saw glowing green stones embedded in the cave walls. They looked the same as the stone that was embedded in Snake's wristband. He knelt down and, with a rock, chipped one of the green stones from the wall, placing it in his pocket. He then continued following the passage until he came across a large stone wall that blocked his path. The wall was arched like it was a secret passage. And it was decorated by rings of strange green symbols that spiraled inward, ending at a hole in the centre.

"What now?" Jason mumbled.

8. THE MASK

8. THE MASK

It's said that all people wear an invisible mask, and only those truly close to someone can see through it.

K ara jumped as the sound of grinding gears and rocks smashing against each other began to fill the room. She turned, and the altar began to descend. She watched as it sank until it was in the dead centre of a giant stone gear. The gear began turning, and the altar started to flip completely around. She watched as the gear and the altar then began to rise toward her, stopping exactly in front of her and rejoining with the stone steps. Now in place of the altar there stood a stone shrine that held a glowing jade eye mask. Kara stood stunned and then turned back around to see that the reapers had halted their advance. Instead, they raised their arms as if worshipping the mask. Kara turned back toward the mask, feeling some kind of pull toward it, hearing a whisper of wind coming from it. Before she realized it, she was drenched in a cold sweat; the mask seemed to be chilling her to the bone. Sullivan had turned his incessant barking into a nasty snarl toward the mask; he too seemed to feel an evil presence coming from it. Kara found herself reaching for the mask and pulled back, pushing her hand on the stone button by the shrine instead. The gear rotated in reverse, and the shrine began to descend and transform back into the altar. As it did, Kara turned to see the reapers beginning to retreat, seemingly fleeing into the dark tunnels from which they had come. Kara took a relieved breath of air. She hadn't realized she had been holding it the whole time.

"Let's go, Sullivan," she said, walking down the steps on shaky legs.

Jason placed his hands on one of the stone rings and pushed up as hard as he could, rotating it counter-clockwise as far as his strength would allow, slowly aligning the green symbols with the ones that matched. Jason then staggered back, his strength beginning to fail him.

"Are these things getting heavier?" he mumbled

between deep breaths. He walked back over to the door and, on a hunch, placed the green stone he had found only moments ago into the centre. His hunch worked. The stone door began to sink into the stone below, creating small tremors throughout the cave. The shaking ceased, and a new pathway was revealed. Jason laughed in relief and sat down for a moment to rest, though he knew he couldn't rest for long.

"Where's Snake?" he asked himself, looking back down the tunnel that he had just come from. He paused for a moment on the shadows. They seemed almost to be shifting, creeping around the corner, threatening to lunge at him like a snake stalking its prey. A chill crawled down his spine, and he decided to get moving again.

Jason reached down and began chipping another green stone from the wall, pocketing it as he had the last one.

"Just in case I need this for later …" Jason mumbled to himself, standing up and making his way back through the tunnel. Jason arrived at the clearing in the centre of the cave, meeting up with Kara and Sullivan, who had both arrived as well.

"Jason, you're alive!" Kara called, running up to him and hugging him tightly.

"Whoa! Hey, Kara, I'm glad you're—" Jason began

but stopped midsentence when his hand got blood on it. "You're bleeding?" he cried, placing his hands on her shoulders and holding her back so he could look into her eyes.

"I'm fine right now, Jason. We've got to get out of here before reapers come," she replied. Jason, though still worried, agreed. The three of them made their way back through the bottom tunnel by the underground pond, taking a few twists and turns as they traversed the dank, dark labyrinth of the cave.

"Jason, the mask—it's pure evil; we have to get rid of it," Kara explained to him as she recalled the dark feeling she had felt from it.

"The mask? Isn't that what Snake was mumbling about?" Jason replied, taking a sharp right turn.

"Snake … when was he talking about that?" Kara replied, and Jason gave her a quick glance.

"When we were fighting before I fell," Jason explained slowly. As he spoke he realized that Kara most likely had been knocked out when Snake threw her against the wall. "Oh, sorry," he muttered.

"The reapers were worshiping it like it was their leader or god or something," Kara replied, getting back to her point.

"That sounds sort of like what Snake was saying. He was bitten by zombies, and this green stone managed to keep him … alive? But he was saying that the mask whispered to him, commanded him," Jason concluded, still not sure if *alive* was the right word to use for what Snake had become. The two then found themselves at a dead end, the path blocked by steel mesh.

"Great. What now?" Jason muttered, throwing his hands into the air. Kara sat down, holding her head with her hands, and Sullivan walked over and began licking her face. Jason then spotted four loose bolts in the corners of the mesh fence.

"Aha, I've got it!" he exclaimed, reaching for one of the bolts and untwisting it.

"Why are they loose?" Kara asked, and Jason looked back at her as he continued untwisting the last of the bolts.

"Don't you get it? It's a secret passage! This mall has been built into and around the caves, so they put secret passages everywhere!" Jason exclaimed, finishing the last bolt. As he did, he fell through the doorway and into the hospital's staff room.

"I'm in," he called, his face against the floor. Kara peeked in and stepped through the steel locker, going over Jason as she carefully entered the room. Jason stood up, cracked his back, and then gave the room a quick look around.

"I hate hospitals. Adding a horror movie theme with real flesh-eating zombies doesn't help with that," Jason said, taking a seat on one of the lounge chairs.

"Let's find some medical supplies," Kara suggested, opening some drawers. Jason remembered that Kara was hurt and jumped off the chair to give her a hand.

"Let's hope we don't find the doctor," Jason joked in an attempt to get Kara to smile. She gave him a faint smile, and he knew she was starting to feel bad. Jason patted himself down, recalling that he didn't have any weapons either, and Kara's handgun was also gone. All they had left was her sniper rifle and Sullivan's fangs to defend themselves. Jason knelt down by Sullivan and began checking him over, also recalling that he had been shot at. But he looked fine. Jason's stomach then growled at him, and he fell back onto his butt.

"Today's looking like shit!" he cursed, standing and walking over to Kara. Kara had found the emergency medical pack and had begun to patch herself up quite sloppily.

"Need help?" Jason asked, taking the kit from her. She nodded and lowered her arms so he could help.

"Where did you learn to patch people up?" she asked, and he shrugged.

"The same place I learned everything else. My

father was a soldier, and he taught me some things," Jason replied, finishing the bandaging.

"Thank you, Jason," she said quietly, staring up at him. Jason could feel the tension; it was the perfect moment for him to kiss her. He could see in her eyes that she knew it too. He gulped and waited for a moment and then began to move in. They were interrupted by Sullivan's barking and a loud bang against the door. Jason pulled away and saw a bloodied female nurse smashing against the door.

"Creepy," he muttered and ripped off a chair leg and signaled Kara to open the door. She reached over and twisted the door handle, and the zombie did the rest. It charged in at the first thing it saw. Sullivan, reacting quickly, grabbed onto the zombie's leg and tripped it, holding on tightly. Jason then took advantage and smashed the zombie's head like a pumpkin. Jason tossed the splintered, bloody chair leg aside and wiped his forehead.

"We should get going," he suggested, and Kara agreed, grabbing a scalpel off the nearby counter. Jason reached down and tore off another chair leg to use, then rubbed Sullivan's head. The three of them exited the room and entered the hospital's top-floor hallway.

9. CORNERED

You never truly understand how hard someone will fight until you corner them.

Jason glanced up at the lights, which had begun to flicker, and cursed to himself as he picked up his pace. He wouldn't allow himself to be trapped in a pitch-dark, bloody hospital with flesh-eating zombies around every corner.

"We should go faster," Jason suggested, pushing a bent stand out of his way. Kara nodded in response, feeling tense about the situation herself. Jason turned and stepped around a corner. A loud squeal caught his attention, and he turned to see a grey-skinned, rotting zombie in a patient's gown charging at him from the other end of the hallway. Its scream attracted others, who began to bash on the windows of their rooms, trying to escape into the hallway. Jason, with the bottom of the chair leg in his hand, smashed the

72

charging zombie on the top of its head hard enough to damage its brain. The ghoul staggered back, its brain not fully destroyed yet. It charged again, and Kara stepped in, jamming her scalpel through its temple. The ghoul's body went limp, and Kara pulled her blade out.

"Let's go!" Jason called, grabbing her wrist and pulling her along behind him as the other zombies began escaping their rooms. Sullivan jumped to follow, nearly outpacing them as he ran from the frenzied zombies. Jason knew they couldn't take them in the condition they were in, not without proper weapons or ammunition. Jason pulled Kara into one of the empty patient rooms, letting Sullivan in and closing the door. He then held his breath as he looked out the window, watching as a small group of blood-covered, torn-up zombies shuffled by. One of them stopped and placed its bloody hand on the window, seemingly looking in with a blank stare. Kara covered her mouth, and Jason pushed on Sullivan's snout to keep him quiet. The zombie gazed in for what seemed like forever before finally turning and shuffling off. Jason finally let his breath out and fell back onto his butt.

"Jason, we need a plan. Where are we going?" Kara asked, and Jason looked over his shoulder at her.

"How should I know?" he whispered back. Kara bit

her lip and leaned back against the wall as she tried to come up with something.

"Food is all I can think about right now. We haven't eaten the whole day," Jason grumbled. Kara sat up straight and raised her index finger.

"The lobby has vending machines," she said out loud, and Jason covered her mouth and hushed her.

"Sorry," she whispered in a muffled voice. Jason moved into a kneeling position and glanced out the window, making sure she hadn't been heard.

"That sounds like a plan, and know what's even better? The exit is by the lobby too," Jason replied and lowered his hand from Kara's mouth. He walked over and opened the door slowly, leaning out to check the hallways. There were a few zombies lurking about, seemingly posted there by the other zombies as lookouts. But that kind of behavior suggested a higher level of intelligence and cooperation than the zombies typically had.

"Stragglers," Jason muttered. If they were caught, Jason knew it would be bad. He crept out and gave Kara the signal to follow. Sullivan tailed Kara and stopped to stare at the zombie standing in the hall. He went to bark, but Kara tugged on his collar, yanking him around the corner. Jason then turned another corner and carefully slipped past a zombie that was checking out a patient's room. Kara went to sneak by in the same way, and Sullivan chomped down on the zombie's leg. Kara cursed and jumped to her feet, jabbing her knife through the zombie's brain before it could make a sound.

"Bad Sullivan!" she hissed. Jason smirked and shook his head. The natural comedy of the situation was easing the tension a bit, but he knew he had to stay focused. One wrong move, one wrong turn or loud noise was all it would take, and they would be surrounded without a place to go. And that wasn't how Jason wanted things to end. He took a deep breath and peeked around the corner—nothing. He gave the signal and crept around the corner, keeping low and away from the windows. Kara jumped when a zombie bashed its own face against the window just above her head. She stopped and waited for a bit, and the zombie turned and walked off. She could feel her heart racing, the tension in the air building. It was thick enough to cut with a knife.

"Found the stairs," Jason whispered breathlessly. The three of them slipped around the last corner and made a dash for the emergency stairs. As they arrived, a zombie stepped around the corner in front of them. Its eyes widened, and its jaw clenched open. It then gave a blood-chilling shriek that echoed throughout the halls. Jason cursed and kicked the zombie, sending it flying to the ground. Sullivan then pinned it down and tore its head right off. Jason turned to see a swarm of flesh-hungry monsters charging at them from mere metres away.

"Go!" he screamed, pushing Kara and Sullivan through the door into the emergency staircase and closing the door tightly. He then knocked over a stand to keep the door shut, knowing that one of them had to stay behind and stall or they wouldn't make it.

"Jason, no—don't do this!" Kara screamed, banging on the window.

"I'm sorry, Kara. One of us has to make it out," he replied, his voice wrenched with pain and terror. He then turned and, once more yelling at her to go, smashed a zombie's head with his wooden chair leg, shattering the chair leg in the process. Kara watched as he turned and made a run down the hallway with a dozen zombies chasing him. Kara clenched her hands tightly and fought back burning tears. She took several sharp breaths and tore herself away from the door, following Sullivan down the stairs.

Jason ran as fast as he could down the hall, taking a sharp turn to the right and leaping over a small metal table on wheels. He stopped and lifted it up, tossing it at his pursuers. It only seemed to stall them for a short moment before they found their ground and continued the chase. Jason, nearly exhausted and out of energy, began to slow down. He opened the door ahead of him and staggered through it, closing it tight behind him and knocking over the nearby filing cabinet. Breathless, he fell back onto his butt and crawled backward away from the violently shaking door. He saw the door begin to chip and splinter, and the window was beginning to crack.

"It's over … Kara, please make it out!" he said to himself between deep breaths. Jason stood up and began searching the room for a weapon, deciding that if today was to be the day he died, he wasn't going out without a fight. He reached over for a golden trophy award, and when he pulled on it, the bookcase began to rotate. Jason, startled, began to look around. He was on the other side of the bookshelf in a poorly lit hallway with old, rusted pipes clinging to the walls. The air was thick with dust and had an old, musty smell, and the light had an orangey-red tint. Jason heard the door on the other side of the bookshelf get smashed apart and could hear the ghouls pour into the office room. He held his breath as he listened to them search the room. He jumped when the bookshelf vibrated from one of them falling over on it. He then waited a moment longer, and there was nothing but the faint sound of the zombies shuffling out of the room.

He took a deep, tension-relieving breath and leaned back against the nearest scaly wall. He closed his eyes and allowed himself to rest for a short moment. After a while, he stood up and took a big step down into the dank, dark tunnel. When he did, his foot splashed into an inch of murky water that coated the tunnel's floor. He clenched his eyes shut in disgust and then started walking into the near darkness, his trail lit only by dying orangey-red bulbs.

Kara made it down to the lobby and, seeing it was clear, stepped in. Her first destination was the vending machine, then out of the hospital and back into the east wing of Cosmic City. She was seething by this point, rage and sorrow building up inside her, tempting her. She knelt down and began to pet Sullivan's head, her tears finally beginning to pour down her cheeks.

"I'm sorry, buddy, but you have to stay here, okay? You can't come where I'm going," she sobbed. She then stood up, gripped her scalpel, and drew her sniper rifle. She told Sullivan to stay and then stepped through the hospital doors, walking into the centre of the east wing. A zombie noticed her and let out a shriek to all of the other zombies in the area. They all rushed her, and Kara aimed her gun at them. She began to unload her entire clip of ammo, taking the zombies' heads with every shot, but it wasn't enough. Kara pulled the trigger again and heard a click. She was out of ammo. Kara dropped her gun and raised her scalpel. She then lost her strength and dropped it, giving up inside.

"Kara, don't!" Jason called, jumping in front of her, raising the blade from the ground, and dispatching the two zombies closest to them. Stunned, Kara stared wide-eyed at him, repeating his name over and over.

"Jason, Jason, how did you—" she said, and he gripped her shoulders.

"I'll tell you at a better time. Let's go!" he said, cutting her off. Sullivan spotted Jason and, with a bark and wag of his tail, rushed out to greet him. Jason then took Kara's hand and, with Sullivan by his side, made a dash down the hall, heading north …

10. I Need a Gun II

10. I NEED A GUN II

History reeks with irony. Guns were first invented to stop senseless wars ... now they're a war's best friend.

"Stop, Jason!" Kara demanded, tugging on his arm. "How did you survive? Were you bitten?" Jason raised his hands in surrender and turned around.

"Okay, I'll tell you now," he began, checking around for zombies before he continued. "First of all, I wasn't bitten, and second, I managed to escape through a secret escape tunnel that had been built into some important doctor's office," he explained, and she raised her eyebrow.

"Why was there a secret tunnel in some doctor's office?" she asked, and Jason smirked.

"I only caught a glimpse of them, but ... he wasn't just some doctor; he was the big guy. I caught a glimpse of some papers on his desk, and I think he was the one doing tests and studies on these things," Jason said, excitement building in his voice.

"But there weren't any zombies before the outbreak, were there?" Kara asked, and Jason shrugged.

"Then what else would a doctor need a creepy escape tunnel behind a bookshelf for?" Jason asked with a smirk, and Kara covered her face with her hands.

"All right," Kara said, lowering her hands. "So then why do you sound so excited?" she asked, and Jason laughed.

"Because so much more has been unveiled, and we're still just circling. Look, you said that you felt some kind of evil emanating from the mask, right? And Snake mumbled something about being connected to it, so it wouldn't be a far stretch to think that the mask is somehow what's causing it. And from the SPU bunker, we also found out that the mall was built over top of the cave like a cover-up. Maybe they found out about the mask, that the green stone somehow makes you an intelligent zombie, and they wanted to market it for money? It makes sense. We know so much more than when we started, and yet—" Jason paused his rant when he heard the mall's speakers crackle to life,

"Attention all personnel, this is the SPU. If you're

alive out there, anywhere, please make your way to the roof. We have a chopper waiting for you and are standing by. We will wait one hour. Repeat ..."

"The SPU is here? Jason, we can get out!" Kara exclaimed and hugged Jason tightly.

"Kara," Jason began, taking her shoulders with his hands and holding her back a little so he could look into her eyes, "what if it's a trap? They could gun us down in an instant!"

"It wasn't the SPU that was trying to kill us earlier—it was the military!" Kara reasoned with him. Jason mulled over it for a moment and then smiled back at her.

"All right, we can check it out. But first I need a gun just in case things go south," he said, and she nodded, happy with the answer. Jason then turned and continued walking north. Jason opened the door that connected the north and east wings together, allowing Kara and Sullivan to enter before checking closely to see if they were being followed. He saw some zombies farther down the east wing. They were standing still. Jason got the notion that they were watching him, but he quickly shook the thought from his mind. *That's impossible,* he thought as he continued looking. He then thought he saw Snake kneeling in the plants on the next level up, glaring down at him with his psychotic eyes, but in an instant he was gone. Jason shook his head, figuring he had started to see things.

"Let's go, Jason!" Kara called, and Jason closed the door finally. He turned and started down the hall. The two stopped when they heard Sullivan whimper. Kara knelt down beside him and began petting him softly.

"Are you hungry too, buddy?" she asked, and he began licking her hands as she petted him. "Jason, we can't keep going like this. Our strength is going to fade," she said to him as her stomach began to growl. Jason sighed deeply, knowing she was right.

"We might find some food at the military base," Jason said, and Kara stood up.

"Military base?" she snapped. "Why do you think we'll find a military base here?"

"Because there's no way that they can run an operation this big without some kind of control centre, and that's where we'll find guns and food," Jason explained, sounding deeply sure of himself.

"And they're not going to shoot us?" she asked sarcastically. Jason shrugged, waving his hands as if trying to wave away the question.

"I'm working on it!" he replied with confidence and then turned and continued down the corridor. He opened the door and allowed Kara and Sullivan out before closing the door and moving a stand in front of it.

"What are you doing?" Kara whispered.

"Trying to hide the door," Jason replied, and she rolled her eyes. They both stopped when Sullivan's barking and the smell of smoke filled the air. They turned to see a massive fire. There were armoured Hummers, tents, and supply crates burning and dead soldiers scattered around.

"Damn it, we can't search the base anymore!" Jason cursed. He punched the stand he had been pushing and then held his hand and shook it in pain.

"Why not? We can avoid the fire," Kara said, taking a step toward the base. Jason caught her arm.

"It's too dangerous. If an ammo pile gets caught in the blaze, the bullets will go everywhere. And there's the chance we'll get trapped in the blaze and burn to death," Jason said. Kara raised an eyebrow at him.

"Wow, what movie did that come from?" she asked, and he smirked at her.

"I don't know, but it sounded pretty awesome right?" he asked, his smirk growing into a grin. She smiled and shook her head and then followed Jason's lead as he approached some of the scattered bodies around the base. He knelt down beside a dead soldier, searching him and finding a handgun—a Beretta M9—and an assault rifle, another SCAR-H. He also found an energy bar and laughed at the irony. They wanted food and weapons, and there it was. The two of them then checked the other two bodies nearby and found similar supplies. Jason sat down and took a big bite of the energy bar, nearly moaning at the pleasure of being able to eat something. Kara opened Sullivan's first and set it on the floor for him to eat and then went after hers as savagely as Jason.

"Yep, zombies must be hungry all the time—that's why they eat like they do," Jason said with a mouth full of food. Kara smiled and nodded and then took another bite. Jason reached over and took a water canteen from the deceased soldier beside him and drank deeply from it. He then passed it to Kara, who drank her share and poured the rest onto the tile floor for Sullivan to lap up. Jason was about to take another bite when he heard the speakers ring loudly before another announcement. At first he heard screams and gurgling noises, and then he heard a man talking.

"Oh, little piggy, I'm still alive!" Jason's eyes widened as he heard Snake laugh. "If you want the answers you're looking for, why don't you come find me!"

Jason sprung to his feet, looking around warily. "How did he know what we were saying?" Jason mumbled. Kara called, and he turned. A pack of limping zombies were moving toward them. Jason zeroed in on them, getting a tingling sensation at the back of his mind. *Are those the zombies from the other side of the corridor?* he thought, a chill shooting through him.

"We should go," Kara said, and Jason nodded, turning and leading the group away from the zombies.

"Kara, what did you mean about the mask being evil and that we should destroy it?" Jason asked as he led them toward the stairway.

"It's like we discussed earlier—the mask seemed to be controlling them. I don't know, but … it seems to break the rules of logic," Kara replied.

Jason chuckled. "I think that logic was broken when zombies started eating people," he said.

"Well, what about the mask?" Kara asked, and Jason turned to her.

"Whatever is going on, whatever this is, it's all connected to that mask. You're right—we need to destroy it. But that's the thing: we're also not heroes. We're normal people caught in an abnormal situation, forced to survive. I've seen every zombie movie and read all the books and guides, and they all say not to be a hero, to only focus on surviving!"

"Where are you going with this, Jason?"

"I'm about to break that rule. Instead of surviving, I'm seeking. I have to go stop Snake. I owe it to Brody," Jason said firmly.

"Wait—*I*? No, Jason, we have—"

"You can't go with me this time. He might kill you," Jason replied, taking her hand.

"He could kill you too," Kara pointed out. Jason smiled weakly at her, and she knew she couldn't change his mind.

"It's something I have to do. Kara, I need you to hold off the zombies with Sullivan so we don't get cornered while fighting Snake. If we both fight him, he'll win."

Kara looked over her shoulder at the oncoming zombies, knowing that he was right—that someone had to even the numbers out.

"What about finding the answers?" she asked.

"The answers lie with Snake and the mask. One way or the other, we will find what we need," Jason replied. Kara stared up into his eyes, and he stared back at hers. Jason then leaned in and kissed her deeply.

"See you when I get back," he said and pulled himself away from her and sprinted up the staircase. Kara turned back around and, with Sullivan at her side, readied herself for waves of flesh-eating monsters to come at her …

11. The Answers

11. THE ANSWERS

In one form or another, we're all seeking answers. Truths. An end to a beginning. Answers lead to truth, and truth leads to light.

The sound of gunfire rang through the air. Over and over, Kara pulled the trigger, and zombies hit the ground as they marched their way over to her. She wiped her brow and dropped her third clip of ammo. As she did, Sullivan leapt at one of the zombies flanking her right side.

"Good boy," she said and reached for another clip of ammo … but she was out. "Damn it!"

She dropped her rifle and pulled out her handgun, letting loose a few rounds into the cloud of flesh. The zombies were completely undeterred by their forces dropping before their eyes, seeming to only care about one thing—her. One of the ghouls got close, and she swung at its neck with her axe, cutting it clean off. She took a few steps back, taking note of what directions they were coming from. Left, right, front ... there was no way out and too many angles to cover.

"Jason, please hurry!" she cried out.

Jason turned and started heading up his last flight of stairs. He reached the top and kicked the door in. he then caught himself on the wall for support as he caught his breath. The feel of cool, fresh air began to rejuvenate him, and he took the chance to look around. He was on the roof of Cosmic City and could see for miles out. To his right was the helipad with a black helicopter decorated in SPU soldier corpses. Jason stepped out from behind the door and glared over at Snake, who was sitting carelessly in the back of the helicopter, smirking maliciously.

"Hey, little piggy, you made it! Oh, and by the way, that comment about me seeing you—I can see everywhere." Snake laughed, waving his large knife around. Jason stopped and thought for a moment, glancing over his shoulder at the staircase.

"Wait, you ... you can see through *their* eyes, can't you?" Jason asked, and Snake snorted at him.

"You finally figured it out, little piggy. Their eyes are my eyes as well—it's like we're all linked together. One mind, one body," Snake explained as he slowly stood up.

"I can control them … to an extent. Zombies are a lot like people—sheep, every last one of them, waiting to be herded. But enough of the small talk, little pig. I know what you're really here for!" Snake chuckled as he walked down the steps, stopping when he was level with Jason.

"Answers," Jason replied, and Snake snorted in response, throwing his arms in the air.

"Revenge," Snake growled deeply, giving Jason a psychotic glare. Snake then lunged at Jason, stabbing at his heart but missing as Jason stepped to the side and brought his knee into Snake's gut. Jason then swung into a left hook, catching Snake by the nose and throwing him back a bit. Snake stumbled back, but Jason was relentless, aiming his assault rifle and pelting Snake's chest with a few bullets. Snake took one last step back and then stared up at Jason and wiped his bloody nose with his hands, giving him an amused smirk. He threw his hands in the air again and shook his head.

"I didn't even feel that, bro." Snake laughed. Jason went to fire again, but Snake stepped in and shoved the gun aside, punching Jason hard in the gut and disarming him. Snake then tossed the gun over the safety railing and off the roof.

"I'm going to kill you slow, piggy," Snake growled. He punched Jason in the face, throwing him sideways. Jason held his hand over his face and backed away.

"How are you still in control?" Jason asked, glaring over at Snake.

"I thought I showed you already—my little green friend. I don't know how or why, but I have the powers of a zombie but the mind of a human. I'm chosen!" Snake laughed, dubbing himself as he held his arms high and stared off at the blue sky.

"I knew it!" Jason snapped. "That's why I couldn't hurt you before. Zombies don't feel pain!"

"Oh, but little pig, I can hurt you," Snake replied.

Jason clenched his jaw and then charged Snake, tackling him to the ground. Jason sat up and began pummelling Snake's face, stopping when Snake just laughed.

"How many times do I have to say it? I don't feel a thing!" Snake screamed out, catching Jason's fist mid-punch.

"That doesn't mean I can't deal damage!" Jason replied, and Snake gritted his teeth, grabbing Jason by the collar and head-butting him. Jason held his face and staggered back away from Snake.

"You want answers?" Snake screamed, dashing forward and catching Jason with a sleeper hold. "You already have your answers. I know you know it—after all, I had the zombies lead you to them!" Snake declared as Jason struggled to get free of the sleeper hold he was trapped in. Jason thought back to the SPU files, the bunker, and the hospital records he had found.

"That's right, little pig," Snake said, staring down at Jason. "This entire outbreak was planned since the creation of Cosmic City. It was released as an attempt to both weaponize the virus and create an elixir of eternal life using the jade mask and the zombies' most special trait: we ... don't ... die!" Snake growled in Jason's ear. Jason gritted his teeth and, with all his strength, pushed backward, sending both of them flying over the safety railing behind them and tumbling down the slanted glass roof below. Jason was the first to catch himself. He stood up quickly and dashed for his gun. He then turned and got tackled by Snake, who held him down and punched him in the face.

"OnLast built this paradise so that it could be turned into the devil's playground. For money, greed, and power." Snake raised his fist for another punch. "Now you have your answers. It's time to join your brother ... oh, and don't worry about your girlfriend. Me and her are going to have a fun time together," Snake said sinisterly. He then went to punch Jason again, but as he did a wave of green light came bursting from somewhere down below, washing over Jason and throwing Snake backward toward the edge of the roof. Jason shook his head and turned over, pushing himself up and onto his feet. He wiped the blood from his mouth and looked over at Snake, who was staring down, perplexed, at himself. His skin was tanned again, his veins were no longer black, his wounds were gone, and his green stone was no longer glowing. Snake stood up, staring down at his hands, and then looked up with anger at Jason.

"What did you do?" he hissed, and Jason smirked. Snake lunged for Jason, but Jason stood his ground, catching Snake's fist and punching him away. Jason then brought his gun up and planted two shots into Snake's chest. Snake placed his hand over his bleeding wound and stared up in shock.

"Goodbye, little pig," Jason said, tapping the trigger and blasting Snake in the head. Snake's head flung back, and he stood on the edge of the roof, stiff as a board, until finally he fell backward off the roof. Jason dropped his gun and turned around, taking a deep gasp for air, relaxing his tense shoulders. He then slowly walked back down the steps, heading for Kara. She turned around as the door opened behind her.

"Jason, you're all right!" she called, running over to him.

"It's over, Kara. It's finally over," Jason replied, linking his fingers with hers and resting his head on her forehead.

EPILOGUE

EPILOGUE

"Now where?" Kara asked quietly as Jason stared out the window of the helicopter they were being escorted in.

"I don't know, Kara," Jason replied, taking her hand in his. "Maybe someplace quiet."

They both jumped when Sullivan came up and began licking their faces.

"We'll have to take Sullivan along!" Kara laughed, petting the dog's head. Jason smiled wide and laughed.

"Yes, we will," he said and turned back toward the window. Kara shifted beside him and stared out, watching the golden sunset with him.

The truth will guide you. It will lie to you, and it will follow you wherever you go. Only the victor's truth is told? I don't believe that. What I do believe is that truth is like a light, and no matter how dark the tunnel, it will always shine through. Follow the light.